Jake
and the
Copycats

A Yearling First Choice Chapter Book

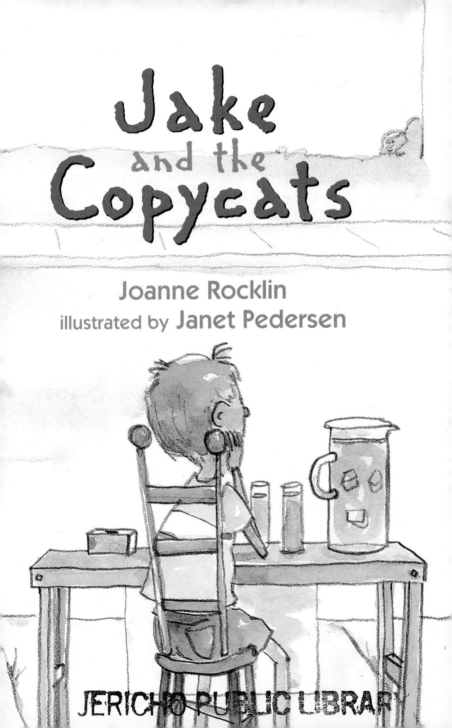

Jake
and the
Copycats

Joanne Rocklin

illustrated by Janet Pedersen

For Michael
—*J.R.*

For Ruthie, Henry, Ben, and Lottie
—*J.P.*

Published by
Bantam Doubleday Dell Publishing Group, Inc.
1540 Broadway
New York, New York 10036

Library of Congress Cataloging-in-Publication Data
Rocklin, Joanne.
  Jake and the copycats / Joanne Rocklin ; illustrated by Janet Pedersen.
    p. cm.
  Summary: Jake is tired of his copycat little brother, Pete, until the day
when Pete's help is required in the rescuing of Jake's cat.
  ISBN 0-385-32530-4 (hardcover).—ISBN 0-440-41408-3 (pbk.)
  [1. Brothers—Fiction. 2. Behavior—Fiction. 3. Cats—Fiction.]
I. Pedersen, Janet, ill. II. Title.
PZ7.R59Jak 1998
[E]—dc21
                                                              97-28799
                                                                  CIP
                                                                   AC

Hardcover: The trademark Delacorte Press® is registered in the U.S. Patent
and Trademark Office and in other countries.
Paperback: The trademark Yearling® is registered in the U.S. Patent and
Trademark Office and in other countries.
The text of this book is set in 17-point Baskerville.
Manufactured in the United States of America
November 1998
10 9 8 7 6 5 4 3 2 1

Contents

1.
A Summer Day

"Nothing to do around here.

Bo-ring," said Jake Biddle.

"Bo-ring," said his brother, Pete.

"Go outside and play,"

said Mrs. Biddle.

"Who can I play with?" asked Jake.

"My best friend, Max, is away!"

"Play with your brother,"

said Mrs. Biddle.

"He's a baby," said Jake.

Jake did a somersault off the couch.

Pete did a somersault off the couch.

"He's a copycat, too," said Jake.

Outside, Jake flopped down
under the lemon tree.
Pete flopped down beside him.
"Move over," said Jake. "You stink."
"*You* stink," said Pete.
"You double stink," said Jake.
"*You* double stink," said Pete.
"Triple stink," said Jake.
"Triple stink," said Pete.
"Quadruple stink," said Jake.
"Quadruple stink," said Pete.
Jake did not know what came next.
"Copycat," he said.

Just then Jake's cat, Fanny, walked by.
"My cat is the smartest cat
on the planet Earth!" said Jake.
"Not on the whole *planet*!" said Pete.
"In the whole universe," said Jake.
"On Mercury, Venus, Mars, Jupiter,
Saturn, Uranus, and Pluto, too."
Jake had learned lots of things
in first grade.

There is one more planet,
thought Jake.
He could not remember it.
But Pete would not know
there was one more planet.
Pete had not learned about planets
in kindergarten.

11

"Fanny can do tricks," said Jake.

Jake snapped his fingers.

"Roll over, Fanny!" said Jake.

Fanny rolled onto her back.

"She just wants her tummy scratched,"
said Pete.

"Stay, Fanny," said Jake.

Fanny stayed.

"Ha! Some trick," said Pete.

He tossed a twig near Fanny.

"Fetch, Fanny!" Pete called.

Fanny yawned at the twig.

"Cats don't fetch," said Jake.

"Everybody knows that."

"Ha! The smartest cat
in the universe would fetch,"
said Pete.

"You stink," Jake said.

"*You* stink," said Pete.

Jake and Pete chased each other
around the lemon tree.
They had a somersault race.

They sprayed each other
with the garden hose.

Then they flopped down beside Fanny.

Mrs. Biddle came outside.

She had ice cream bars
and lemonade.

"Having fun?"
Mrs. Biddle asked.

"Sort of," said Jake.

"Sort of," said Pete.

2.
Jake's Good Ideas

Jake had a good idea.

He picked a lemon.

He squeezed lemon juice

into a pitcher.

He found some cranberry juice

and apple juice in the refrigerator.

He poured cranberry juice

and apple juice into the pitcher, too.

He added ice cubes

and four mashed

strawberries.

Then Jake made a big sign.

JAKE'S SUPER FRUIT PUNCH
10 CENTS

He carried everything outside.

"Can I help?" asked Pete.

"Does the sign say

'Jake *and Pete's* Super Fruit Punch'?"

Jake asked.

Pete looked at the sign.

He checked every word.

"No," Pete said.

"Then you can't help," said Jake.

Pete went into the house.

Soon he came out again.

JAKE'S SUPER
FRUIT PUNCH
10 cents

"Copycat," said Jake.

"Uh-*uh*!" said Pete.

"I used five strawberries.

You only used four."

Along came Alice.

She looked at Jake's sign.

She looked at Pete's sign.

"Too much money," said Alice.

Jake had a good idea.

He jumped up to change his sign.

Pete copied him.

But Pete was too late.

"Terrific punch, Jake," said Alice.

Along came Ricky.

Pete called, "My punch is now on sale for four cents!"

"Mine is three cents!" said Jake.

Ricky bought Jake's punch.

"No fair!" said Pete.

"It is so!" said Jake.

Pete changed his sign again.

But Jake had another good idea.

Now his sign said:

JAKE'S SUPER FRUIT PUNCH
AND A CAT TRICK
1 CENT

Along came Margo.

She was walking her dog, Biff.

Margo read Jake's sign.

"Cats can't do tricks," she said.

"Fanny can," said Jake.

Jake snapped his fingers.

"Roll over, Fanny!" Jake said.

Fanny rolled onto her back.

"She just wants her tummy scratched,"
said Margo. "My dog, Biff, can fetch."
Margo threw a twig.
"Fetch, Biff!" she called.
But Biff did not run after the twig.
Biff ran after Fanny.
"Hiss-s-s!" went Fanny.

Fanny jumped up on the table.

So did Biff.

"What a mess!" said Jake.

Soon Pete said, "I'm all sold out."

"We both need to make
more punch," said Jake.

"And pick more lemons," said Pete.

"I have a good idea," said Jake.

"Let's be partners."

"Sure," said Pete.

And Jake changed his sign
one last time.

JAKE AND PETE'S
SUPER-DUPER FRUIT PUNCH
5 CENTS

3.
Party Babies

It was Pete's birthday.

Pete and Jake waited

for the birthday party guests.

"We're the same age now," said Pete.

"I'm still older," said Jake.

"But we're *both* six," said Pete.

"I'll be in second grade

when the summer is over," said Jake.

"You'll only be in first grade."

"There's no school now," said Pete.

"But—" said Jake.

Just then the doorbell rang.

"Hello," said Otto.

"A first-grade baby," said Jake.

The doorbell rang again.

It was Hannah and Margo.

"More first-grade babies," said Jake.

Along came Ricky and Alice.

"I can't stand it!" said Jake.

"Two more first-grade babies."

Then Cousin Boo-Boo Biddle came.

"A kindergarten baby.

This party stinks!" said Jake.

"I like you, Jake," said Boo-Boo.

"Choose a partner
for the three-legged race!"
called Mrs. Biddle.
"I choose Jake," said Pete.
"We'll win for sure!"
"I'll win *all* the games," said Jake.

Jake and Pete started off strong.

Suddenly—PLOP!

Jake and Pete tripped over a shoelace.

Pete's shoelace.

"Sorry," said Pete.

"I'll tie it tighter this time."

Pete began to tie a double knot.

"Hurry up!" said Jake.

"Done," said Pete. "Now we'll win!"

But it was too late.

"Time for the treasure hunt!"

called Mrs. Biddle.

Everybody got a clue.

"*Wah!* I can't read my clue,"

cried Boo-Boo. "Please help me, Jake."

"'Peek under the doormat,'" read Jake.

Boo-Boo peeked under the doormat.

She found another clue.

"Read this clue, too," Boo-Boo said.

"'Look behind the couch,'" read Jake.

Boo-Boo found another clue

behind the couch.

"Now this one, please," said Boo-Boo.

"'Walk ten paces to the window.

Look under the flowerpot,'" Jake read.

Jake wanted to say,

"Walk ten paces to the closet.
Stay there, Boo-Boo."
He did not have time to read
all his own clues.
"Hurray! I found the treasure!
I like you, Jake," said Boo-Boo.

Now it was time for hide-and-seek.

Jake knew the greatest hiding spot
in the universe.

He could see everybody,
but nobody could see him.

Pete was It.

"Here I come, ready or not!"
Pete said.

Pete found Hannah and Margo
and Ricky and Alice
and Otto and Boo-Boo.

Everybody except Jake.

"Where are you, Jake?" asked Pete.

"Birthday cake!" called Mrs. Biddle.

Jake saw everyone run
to the picnic table
for cake.

Who cares about a baby cake?

thought Jake.

A baby cake with little bears on it.

Probably tastes good, though.

Probably tastes great.

Jake poked his head out.

"Found you!" said Pete.

"Oh, well," said Jake.

"Let's go have some cake."

"I'll blow out my candles
in one big puff!" said Pete.

"Just like you do, Jake."

4.
Hiss-s-s!

At five o'clock
the party guests went home.
Pete and Jake looked at Pete's gifts.
"My Space Hero flashlight
is really cool!" said Pete.
"Thanks again, Jake."

"I knew you'd like it," said Jake.

"I chose it myself."

Jake and Pete put on

their Space Hero caps.

"Space Heroes, away!" shouted Jake.

"Zoom, zoom!" shouted Pete.

Mrs. Biddle came outside.

She was carrying a box.

"I have a gift for you, too,"

she said to Pete.

"My very own kitten!" said Pete.

"Just like Jake."

"What will you call him?" Jake asked.

"Manny," said Pete.

"Copycat!" said Jake.

"Manny sounds like Fanny."

"Then I'll call him Hey-Manny,"
said Pete.

Fanny showed Hey-Manny her teeth.

"Hiss-s-s!" went Fanny.

She looked like a different cat to Jake.

Like a witch-cat.

Or an angry tiger.

"*Hiss-s-s!*" went Fanny again.

She chased Hey-Manny

around the backyard.

She chased Hey-Manny up the tree.

Then Hey-Manny chased Fanny

around the backyard.

Hey-Manny chased Fanny up the tree.

"My cat is a copycat," said Pete.

"Come down, Fanny," called Jake.
But Fanny did not come down
from the tree.

"Hiss-s-s!" went Fanny.

"Let's leave her alone,"
said Mrs. Biddle.

"She'll feel better soon."

It got dark.

Fanny did not come down.

Jake could not sleep.

Fanny must be the loneliest cat
in the universe, he thought.

"I'm thinking about Fanny," said Pete.

"Me too," said Jake.

"I have a good idea," said Pete.

Jake and Pete went outside.

Pete climbed on Jake's shoulders.

Pete shined his Space Hero flashlight up the tree.

"Come down, Fanny," called Jake.

"Come down, Fanny," called Pete.

"Meow," went Fanny.

She came down to Pete and Jake.

"Thanks for your help," said Jake.

"Anytime," said Pete.

Jake looked up at the big, black sky.

He remembered something.

"There are nine planets," said Jake.

"I forgot to tell you about Neptune."

"Thanks," said Pete.

"Anytime," said Jake.